KATE'S
SECRET PLAN

KATE'S SECRET PLAN

*The story of a young Quarter Horse and the persistent
girl who will not let obstacles stand in their way*

Written by **Susan Saunders**
Illustrated by **Sandy Rabinowitz**
Cover Illustration by **Christa Keiffer**
Developed by Nancy Hall, Inc.

SCHOLASTIC INC.
New York Toronto London Auckland Sydney

ISBN 0-590-31658-3

12 11 10 9 8 7 6 5 4 3   8 9/9 0 1 2/0

Printed in the U.S.A.   40

First Scholastic printing, December 1997

CONTENTS

Happy Birthday!

Kate McGill was dreaming about horses: a big, beautiful herd of them, chestnuts and bays and grays. They thundered across the Canadian prairie. Their manes and tails streamed in the wind.

Kate galloped after them. But she was riding lazy old Brownie, so she couldn't keep up. She was falling farther and farther behind . . .

"Come on, Brownie!" Kate urged in her dream. "Faster! Faster!"

Then one of the McGill roosters crowed right under her bedroom window. A dog barked. And Kate

slowly opened her eyes.

A golden sun was floating over the low hills beyond the barn. Kate scrunched down in her bed and pulled the blankets more tightly around herself. It was early June in southern Alberta, Canada. But it was still chilly.

Suddenly Kate remembered what day it was: June 8th, 1926—it was her tenth birthday!

She flung her covers off and hurried to dress. "Happy birthday to me, happy birthday to me!" Kate sang to herself. She zipped up her riding pants and pulled on her western boots. Louder, she added, "Happy birthday to both of us . . ."

"Both of us" meant Kate and Brian. And a couple of knocks on the other side of Kate's bedroom wall told her that Brian had heard the song. It was Brian's tenth birthday, too, because Kate and Brian were twins.

Both of them were tall for their age, and pencil thin. And they both had bright blue eyes, reddish-blond hair, and freckles like their dad.

But Kate and Brian were less alike in other ways.

Kate had always been crazy about horses. Mr. McGill often said that she was born with horse sense.

As a toddler, Kate begged to sit in the saddle in front of her father. She had been riding alone since she was three. That's when her dad plopped her bareback onto George, a poky, fat plow horse. Kate covered lots of miles, steering George round and round the corral.

When she was six, Kate started riding Brownie.

"Brownie is slow, but steady," said Mr. McGill. Which was important when Kate was younger. But now she often wished she had a mount who was livelier.

Brian could ride, too, of course. He helped out with horseback chores on the ranch, like rounding up cattle or riding the fence line to look for breaks in the barbed wire.

Almost daily in the summertime, though, Brian rode straight over to the Frasers' farm. He and Asa Fraser were best friends. And Asa was almost as crazy about baseball as Brian was. They spent every spare moment they could practicing pitching, catching, and batting a baseball.

Brian said that he could take horses or leave them. What he really wanted was to be a baseball player and live in a big city with trolleys and electric lights.

Not Kate. Kate never wanted to live anywhere but on a ranch.

She ran a brush over her hair and smiled at

herself in the mirror. "I'm ready for a birthday!" she said.

She bumped into Brian in the hall.

"What do you think we're getting this year?" he asked as they headed toward the kitchen. "Mom and Dad haven't said one word."

"I couldn't even make Peter give me a hint!" Kate replied.

Peter was the twins' older brother. He would be leaving the ranch soon. He was starting classes at the new university in Edmonton, the capital of Alberta.

"I hope they don't make us wait all day for our presents," said Kate, who wasn't very good at waiting.

"But Dad has to drive to the train. He's picking up the Willises," Brian reminded her. Joe Willis had just been hired as the McGills' new foreman. "Then Mom and Dad will have to get them settled."

Kate groaned: "That'll take up most of the morning. And the afternoon, too. It'll be dark before we have our birthday!"

She pushed open the door to the warm, sunny kitchen.

"Greetings to the birthday girl and boy!" Mr. McGill boomed from his chair at the head of the long wooden table. He was a big man, with curly red hair and twinkly blue eyes.

"Happy birthday, both of you!" said Mrs. McGill. Her dark-brown hair was wound neatly around her head in a thick braid, her heart-shaped face flushed from the heat of the big, black wood stove.

Mrs. McGill gave the twins a hug, leaving Peter tending the griddle.

Peter was tall and thin, like the twins, with dark hair and green eyes like their mother.

"Yeah, happy birthday, squirts," Peter said, flipping a pancake. Then he added it to a huge stack already piled on a platter.

"Yum! Pancakes!" said Brian hungrily.

"With strawberries?" asked Kate. Pancakes with strawberries and whipped cream was just about her favorite meal!

"That's right—we had a few jars of berries left from last summer," said her mother.

Canadian summers are short, so Mrs. McGill jarred and canned as many fresh fruits and vegetables as she could.

"Sit down, children . . . ," said Mrs. McGill.

She bent over the platter of pancakes for a moment. When she turned around, the pancakes were topped with strawberries and whipped cream. And they were decorated with eleven flickering birthday candles, just right for making wishes.

"Ten candles, plus one to grow on!" said Mrs. McGill.

She set the platter down in the middle of the kitchen table.

"Happy birthday to you . . . ," sang Mr. and Mrs. McGill, and Peter said, "Blow out the candles before our pancakes get cold!"

"And make a wish!" said Mrs. McGill.

Kate and Brian both took a deep breath. Then they blew at the same time.

Kate didn't know what Brian had wished for. But she had wished for the same thing for years—a new horse.

"Since we'll be busy with the Willises today . . . ," began Mr. McGill.

Kate and Brian looked at each other and groaned.

" . . . we thought we'd give you your presents as soon as we've eaten. It may be the only free moment we have," said Mrs. McGill. "Is that all right with you two?"

"You bet!" said Brian.

"Oh, yes!" said Kate.

"Let's dig in," said Peter, piling pancakes, strawberries, and whipped cream on each of their plates.

Breakfast was delicious, but Kate hardly tasted it.

She was much too busy trying to imagine what her present from her parents might be.

Maybe a new saddle blanket—her old one was almost worn out. Or a new bridle—she had seen a beautiful headstall with silver buckles the last time they were in Medicine Hat.

Or what if the present was something boring, like a new chest of drawers? Or a bed?

Just a week or two ago, her mother had said, "Kate, your bedroom furniture is older than I am."

"I have a feeling it's furniture," Kate said to herself. And her heart sank.

The Best Gift Ever

Mrs. McGill said, "Well I think it's time for those presents."

"I believe that it's Brian's turn to go first this birthday," said Mr. McGill. The twins took turns opening presents first from year to year.

"In that case . . ." Mrs. McGill hurried into the pantry off the kitchen. She returned with a large square box, which she handed to Brian.

"It's awfully light . . .," said Brian, sounding disappointed. "Is it clothes?"

"Maybe. You'd better open it and see," said his father.

Brian tore the brown paper off the box and pulled

15

it open . . . The box was full of wadded-up newspapers!

Brian's face fell. "Is there anything in here at all?" he asked his parents.

"Just keep looking," said Mrs. McGill.

So Brian dug around in the paper and pulled out a big white envelope.

"That's it . . . ," said his father.

Brian shrugged and opened the envelope.

Inside it was a square of cardboard. A picture of a baseball player was glued to one corner of the cardboard. A newspaper advertisement for an Edmonton hotel was glued to another. An old train ticket from the Canadian Pacific Railways was stuck in the center of the cardboard.

"Is it a puzzle?" Brian asked, looking puzzled himself. "Are these clues?"

"Kind of," said his mother.

"I don't know what a baseball player and a train have to do with each other," said Brian. "And a hotel?"

Peter rolled his eyes. "Let's put you out of your misery," he said to Brian. "Turn it over."

On the back of the cardboard, Mrs. McGill's tiny print explained the gift.

"A baseball game!" Brian shouted as soon as he had read it. "I'm going to a real baseball game—in

Edmonton! This is great!"

"But how will you get there?" Kate asked, since Edmonton wasn't exactly around the corner from the McGill Ranch. In fact, it was hundreds of miles away. Neither she nor Brian had ever been there.

"Brian and I will take the train to Medicine Hat," Mr. McGill said, pointing to the train-ticket clue. "Then we'll switch to the Calgary train, and then to the Edmonton line. We'll stay in a hotel in Edmonton and see a baseball game—maybe two!"

"Peter will go on the train with them and get settled at the university," Mrs. McGill told Kate.

"What about us?" said Kate to her mother, feeling left out.

Baseball tickets weren't that interesting to Kate. But a trip to Edmonton, a stay in a hotel, and a visit to Peter's university certainly were!

"You and I will run the ranch while they're gone," said Mrs. McGill. "Don't you have something for Brian, Kate?"

"Umm." Kate had been thinking about what fun it would be to go to Edmonton. She had almost forgotten her own present for Brian. She pulled an envelope out of her shirt pocket.

Brian opened it, read the note inside, and grinned.

"A present I can always use," he said, holding it

out so that his parents and Peter could see what Kate had written: "Good for two weeks' worth of chores."

"Now you can play ball with Asa all day long if you want," explained Kate.

"Thanks, twin," said Brian.

Peter gave Brian a baseball cap, white striped with blue. "I ordered it from Toronto," Peter told him. "It's the real thing."

Brian tried the cap on and practiced a couple of slow-motion pitches: "This is the best birthday I've ever had!" he exclaimed.

"Kate, I guess you aren't that interested in your present, are you?" teased Mr. McGill.

"Sure I am," said Kate. But how could her present possibly be as exciting as a trip to Edmonton?

"Let's go out to the barn," said Mr. McGill.

The barn: that meant Kate's birthday present was too big to wrap up . . .

"Furniture," Kate mumbled to herself. "I just knew it."

They all trooped out to the barn—even the dogs, Stella and Brutus, joined them.

Mr. McGill led them around to the back of the barn.

The McGills' Model-T Ford was parked outside the barn. Kate almost couldn't believe it, because her dad was so careful with the car.

Brian was surprised, too. "Why is the car sitting out, Dad?" he asked.

But Mr. McGill was saying, "Push open the barn door, Kate. Go ahead . . . "

Kate lifted the latch and slowly slid the door open. She was trying to come up with something nice to say about new furniture. She didn't want her parents to feel bad . . .

Then she stopped dead!

There, in the big box stall under the hayloft, stood a horse. And not just any horse—he was the most beautiful horse Kate had ever seen. He was a golden chestnut—the color of caramel—with a white mane and tail and three white stockings.

"Oh!" was all that Kate could say. "Oooh!"

"He's yours, honey," said Mr. McGill.

"Do you like him?" asked Mrs. McGill.

Did she like him? "I love him!" Kate said breathlessly.

Chinook

Kate held her right hand out, and walked toward the horse. He gazed at her with his warm brown eyes and nickered softly.

"I think he likes you, too," said Mrs. McGill, as the horse stretched out his neck to nibble at Kate's fingers.

When Kate got close enough to stroke him, the horse stood as steady as a rock. Then he rubbed his head against her.

"How old is he? Where did he come from?" Kate asked.

"He's four years old. We got him from a Quarter-Horse breeder north of Medicine Hat," said Mr. McGill.

"Brian will be riding Peppy now, with Peter off at the university. We thought you were ready for a better horse, too."

Peppy was Peter's cutting horse. Peppy and Peter had won the cutting-horse contest at the Medicine Hat fair many times.

In the cutting-horse contest, a horse and rider had only two-and-a-half minutes to show what they could do. During that time, they had to choose a cow or steer out of a herd of cattle. Then the horse's job was to keep that cow from returning to the herd, no matter what. The rider's job was to sit still and let the horse do its best work.

When everything went right, Kate thought there was nothing more beautiful. And there was nothing she would rather do herself than ride a cutting horse at the fair.

But there was one problem—she was a girl. The cutting contest in Medicine Hat was only for grown-up men and boys under eighteen years old. Not girls.

With Peter in college, Brian would be riding Peppy at the rodeo. And Kate didn't think it was fair.

For one thing, Brian wasn't that interested. For another, Peter let Kate cut on Peppy a few times at the ranch. And she knew that she was better at riding him than Brian was.

"There's no use arguing about it, honey," Mr. McGill had said to Kate more than once. "Girls don't ride in the cutting contest."

And Kate always thought, "What can girls do to win trophies, then? Bake pies, or make pickles?"

Her mom was fond of telling her, "Kate, you were born in 1916, a good year for women—the year we got the vote in Alberta." So why was it okay for women to decide who would be running the government, but not okay for them to ride in a cutting-horse contest? It didn't make sense. When Kate thought about it for long, she got angry. She wanted to ride, not cook. And she was too young to vote!

But Kate wasn't going to make herself mad today. Not with this amazing birthday present.

"What's his name?" she asked, her arms around the horse's neck.

"They were calling him Stockings, because of his white legs," said Mr. McGill.

Kate thought for a minute. Then she smiled and said, "I'm going to name him Chinook—a real Canadian name."

A chinook was a warm, dry wind that blew into southern Canada in the wintertime. It was like magic: In the space of a few hours, a chinook could make the temperature rise forty degrees and could melt snow.

Chinook would be a special name for a special horse.

"You're going to like it here, Chinook," Kate said to the horse, stroking his neck.

He bobbed his head as if he were agreeing, and whinnied.

"Hey—you'll have to let go of him long enough to open my present," Peter said to Kate.

He handed her a soft, flat package wrapped in old newspapers.

As soon as Kate tore open a corner of the package, she knew what was inside. "A new saddle blanket!" she exclaimed, tracing the red, black, and cream pattern with her fingers. "Oh, thank you, Peter."

"It's double-thick wool, and it was hand-woven," Peter told her.

"It's perfect," Kate said.

Brian gave Kate a new hatband he had braided himself, out of all different colors of horsehair.

"The white is from Peppy's tail, the black is from Brownie, and the red is from old George," Brian said. He lifted Kate's cowboy hat off her head and removed the old leather band.

Kate slipped on the new one in its place: "It even matches my new saddle blanket. Thank you, Brian."

Kate liked her new blanket and hatband—but she couldn't take her eyes off Chinook.

"Would you like to try him out?" her father suggested.

"Oh, yes," said Kate. She led Chinook to the corner of the barn where the McGills kept their saddles and bridles.

Kate's dad helped her shorten the headstall of a bridle to fit Chinook's head. Quarter Horses have short heads, widely spaced eyes, and perky little ears, and Chinook had the perfect Quarter-Horse head.

While Brian held the reins, Kate folded her new saddle blanket in half. Carefully, she laid it lightly over Chinook's withers. She smoothed the blanket until it was straight, and stepped back to admire the red, black, and cream stripes against her horse's caramel-colored back.

Once the saddle was in place on the saddle blanket, Mr. McGill cinched it up carefully and then checked to make sure it was tight.

"You're all set," he said to Kate.

The rest of the McGills followed Kate as she led Chinook out of the barn toward the big round corral where Peter practiced on Peppy. Chinook had a quick, easy way of walking. His ears were pricked forward as he looked around his new home.

"I think he's smart," Peter said. "He's taking everything in."

Kate climbed into the saddle. She almost couldn't believe it. Yesterday, she was plodding around on old Brownie. Today, she was riding this incredible horse!

"Do some figure eights to see how he reins," her dad said. "But start out slow, Kate."

Kate nodded. She squeezed her legs just the tiniest bit against Chinook's sides, and he immediately moved forward. That was good. It showed that Chinook was ready to do what Kate asked, as soon as she asked him to.

His walk was smooth and easy. Chinook didn't drag his feet the way Brownie sometimes did.

Kate and Chinook made a circle to the right for the first part of the figure eight.

"How about a trot?" Mr. McGill called out.

Kate squeezed her legs a bit tighter and leaned forward, to speed Chinook up. They finished the figure eight in a comfortable trot.

Then she nudged the horse again and loosened up on the reins. Chinook broke into a lope. His strides were even and flowing.

"Like sitting in a rocking chair!" Peter called from the fence.

Suddenly Chinook lifted his head higher. His eyes and ears were trained on something in the distance, past the barn. Part of the McGill cattle herd was coming in to drink water at the stock tank.

"He's watching the cows," Peter said.

"Chinook will make a good cow horse," said Mr. McGill approvingly.

"He'd make a good cutting horse," Kate couldn't help adding.

"Now, Katie . . . "Mr. McGill began.

"I know—only boys ride in the cutting contest," murmured Kate.

Still, as she watched Chinook watching the cattle, she couldn't help wishing things were different.

Mr. McGill checked his pocket watch. "Almost time to pick up the Willises," he said to his wife, and added, "Peter, help me hitch up the wagon."

"Is it all right if I ride over to Asa's?" Brian asked. "I want to tell him about Edmonton."

"I guess so—it's your birthday," said his mother. "But don't bother Mrs. Fraser. And bring Asa back for lunch if you want to."

"I will," said Brian. "Thanks again for the birthday gifts!"

Kate was busy making more figure eights on Chinook. And circles. And stopping him. And starting again.

Mr. McGill and Peter left for the railhead to meet the new foreman and his family. They hitched a wagon to the Model T to carry the Willises' belongings.

Kate hardly noticed they were gone.

She barely heard her mother say that she was going to the cabin to do some last-minute straightening up. "The cabin" is what the McGills called the first ranch house, the one built by Kate's grandmother and grandfather when they had come to Canada from Scotland many years before. Made of huge logs, it was perched on the edge of a small creek a mile or so from the main house. The Willises would be living there now.

Kate gave Chinook a really good workout. Then she walked him around for a few minutes to cool him off before leading him into the barn to unsaddle and groom him.

She was just finishing up, painting hoof oil on Chinook's feet, when the McGills' car drove up outside.

"Emma?" Kate heard her dad call to her mom. "We're here!"

The ranch dogs were barking a greeting. The screen door slammed at the house, which meant her mother was running down the front steps. Kate heard more voices, and then Mr. McGill called out, "Katie, come out here and say hello."

Kate turned Chinook into the box stall, where

there was water and fresh hay for him. Then she hurried outside.

CHAPTER
FOUR

The Willises

The Model T and the wagon were parked in front of the ranch house. The wagon was piled high with trunks and boxes. Peter and Kate's mom and dad were talking to the man and woman who stood beside the car.

The woman held a plump baby in her arms. A dark-haired little girl was pressed against her. Leaning on the back of the wagon was a wiry blond boy. Kate knew he was just a few months older than she and Brian. She hoped he liked to ride better than Brian did—sometimes it was nice to have company on horseback.

The dogs were sprawled beside the boy, thumping

the ground with their tails. Absently, the boy started to scratch Brutus's back with the toe of his boot.

Mr. McGill caught sight of Kate and said, "This is Kate, one of our twins. It is Kate's—and her brother Brian's—tenth birthday today!"

"Well, happy birthday, Kate, and many happy returns!" the woman said. She was short and round, with curly blond hair and an open, friendly face.

"This is Mrs. Willis, Kate," said Mrs. McGill. "And this is Mr. Willis."

Kate shook hands with them both.

Mr. Willis didn't have much to say. He looked stern.

"Maybe he's just sad," Kate thought. Her parents had told her how the Willises moved from the United States to northern Alberta, where they bought a small ranch of their own. But bad luck and hard winters meant they had lost it.

Mrs. Willis wasn't stern, though. She gave Kate a warm smile, and a hug with the arm that wasn't holding the baby. "Please call me Cora," she told Kate.

"This young fellow is Michael," Cora Willis said, gesturing to the baby in her arms, "and our girl is named Mary." Mary smiled shyly at Kate. She had a sprinkling of freckles across her nose and big blue eyes.

"And that there is Jimmy," Mr. Willis said, pointing at the boy leaning against the wagon.

When Jimmy kept scratching Brutus's back without looking up, Mr. Willis added, "Jimmy, come over here and shake hands." Jimmy slouched over to the steps where Kate was standing and stuck his hand out. He still hadn't raised his eyes.

But when Kate said, "Nice to meet you, Jimmy," and put out her own hand, Jimmy's eyes met hers.

Jimmy Willis's eyes were bright green. And they were definitely not friendly. Then he looked quickly away.

"What is that all about?" Kate wondered, uneasy.

But no one else seemed to notice.

"Let's go into the house for lunch," her mom said to the Willises.

"Oh, we couldn't," said Mrs. Willis. "We don't want to trouble you . . ."

"No trouble at all," said Mrs. McGill. "You don't need to start cooking the minute you get to the cabin. And the children must be hungry."

The big round table was already set. Mr. McGill put Mr. Willis in the chair on his right, and Peter on his left.

Brian and Asa Fraser came racing up the front steps and into the house just in time to squeeze in next to Peter at the table.

Jimmy Willis slid into the empty chair beside his father. Mary sat next to Jimmy, and Kate sat beside Mary.

Kate could see Jimmy glancing around the sunny dining room. He studied the photographs of Kate's grandfather and grandmother in their carved wooden frames. He looked up at the oil lamps made of elk horns that hung above the dining-room table, and at the glass-fronted cupboard filled with the McGills' good china. Then he stared at the silver cups and trophies lined up on the mantel above the fireplace.

Mr. Willis noticed them, too. "Are those prizes from Medicine Hat?" he asked Mr. McGill. Kate's dad must have been talking about the contest on their way back from the railhead.

"That's right," said Mr. McGill. "Peter and Peppy have placed in one of the top spots for the last four years." Mr. McGill nodded at Brian, across the table, and went on, "I hope that Brian will add to the collection this summer. Right, son?"

Jimmy's bright-green gaze focused on Brian.

Brian wriggled in his seat, looking a little uncomfortable.

"Yes, sir," he mumbled.

"Why not? If you've got the right horse, it's easy to

34

win," Jimmy suddenly muttered under his breath.

"What?" said his father.

"Nothing," Jimmy said.

But Kate had heard him plainly.

Mrs. McGill and Mrs. Willis had been heaping the table with food from the kitchen: roast chicken, smoked venison, potato salad, pickled green beans, deviled eggs, and dozens of hot rolls. Now they sat down, too, and everyone started serving themselves.

"Have you been having a good birthday, Kate?" Cora Willis asked as she helped Mary with a platter of chicken.

"The best ever!" Kate said. "Mom and Dad gave me a wonderful Quarter Horse! He's four years old, he's the most beautiful color, he's . . ."

But she stopped herself.

"I probably sound like I'm bragging," she thought. She could almost feel Jimmy's cold green eyes drilling into her.

Luckily, Mary said shyly, "I wish I had a horse to ride."

"Mary . . . ," said Cora Willis, shaking her head, ". . . you know we can't afford . . ."

But Kate interrupted her. "Mary, you can ride Brownie. Brownie used to be my horse, and she is one of the nicest horses in the world."

"Can I really?" Mary said, clapping her hands together.

"I promise," said Kate.

"Oh, goody!" Mary said.

Brian turned to Jimmy. "Do you play baseball? Maybe you and Asa and I could . . ."

"I don't have time for games," Jimmy muttered. "I have to help my father."

From the way he said it, it was easy to tell that Jimmy thought Brian and Asa—and Kate, too—rarely did anything but play.

Which was unfair—there were chores to be done every day on a ranch. And Brian, Kate, and Asa Fraser did plenty of them!

Brian's face flushed bright red. Kate knew that it would be a long time before her brother tried to be nice to Jimmy Willis again. She wasn't feeling very friendly toward him herself!

CHAPTER
FIVE

Kate Makes Up
Her Mind

After lunch, Mr. McGill and the Willises prepared to drive over to the cabin. Before they left, though, Mr. McGill said, "Joe, maybe you'd like to take a look at Kate's new horse first."

Mr. McGill, Mr. Willis, Kate, and Jimmy trooped out to the barn to see Chinook. His head was raised and his ears were pricked as they walked up to the box stall.

Mr. Willis nodded approvingly. "That is one good-looking gelding," he said. "Where did you get him?"

"I bought him from a Quarter-Horse breeder outside of Medicine Hat," said Mr. McGill.

Mr. Willis said, "He has a good build for cutting.

Are you going to train him for that?"

Mr. McGill shook his head: "No, this is Kate's horse, to do with as she pleases." Of course, Kate knew what that meant—to do anything other than cutting.

"What if Mr. Willis is right, though?" Kate thought. "Chinook is built for cutting. Doesn't he deserve a chance to prove himself?"

Chinook was certainly built for the quick stops and turns of cutting. His shoulder and hip angles matched, which gave him good balance. His hocks were strong and low to the ground, and his back was short.

Kate had already seen how he watched cattle. She was almost sure he'd been born with what cutting-horse people called "cow-smarts."

"Kate?" Mr. McGill's voice broke into her thoughts. "Mr. Willis wants to know what your plans are for Chinook."

"Are you going to work on his reining?" Mr. Willis asked.

"Oh. Yes. I think so," Kate said.

But Mr. Willis was already saying to her dad, "It's too bad your boy can't ride this fellow in the cutting, too, in the first-timers' class."

"This horse is wasted on a girl," Jimmy Willis

mumbled in a voice loud enough to be heard.

Kate knew the Willises were just saying what most men thought. But she was suddenly furious! Kate was as good a rider as any boy she knew. And she was sure that included Jimmy Willis!

In a split second, Kate made up her mind. She was going to train Chinook to be a cutting horse. And she was going to win the first-timers' trophy in Medicine Hat this summer. She didn't know how yet— she just knew she would do it, even if she had to cut off all her hair to look like a boy!

Kate already knew a lot about how to train Chinook to cut. She had helped her dad cut cattle in the pasture many times. And she had been watching him and Peter train Peppy for the show ring for the last five years. She had even cut on Peppy herself a few times.

Kate would have to train Chinook in secret, though, if she didn't want everyone constantly telling her how silly she was being.

She glanced up to find Jimmy Willis staring at her. Kate stared right back at him, until he looked away.

"Dad, I'd like to ride Chinook in the pasture this afternoon," Kate said to her father then.

"Well . . . all right," said Mr. McGill. "But take it slow at first. If he has any bad habits, I want you to

discover them walking, not running."

"I'll be careful."

The horn on the Model T beeped.

"I guess the women are ready," said Mr. McGill to Mr. Willis. "I'll show you the rest of the ranch tomorrow."

Kate was standing on the porch with her mother when her dad drove away in the Model T with the Willises. She could see Jimmy's thin face peering out the side.

"I don't like him at all," Kate said in a low voice.

"Who don't you like?" Mrs. McGill said, giving her daughter her full attention. "And why?"

"Jimmy Willis," Kate said. "I tried to be friendly. But all I got back from him was mean remarks about girls, and about Chinook, and . . ."

"Kate, you have to remember what Jimmy's been through recently, losing the ranch," said Mrs. McGill. "Think about what he's had to give up besides the ranch itself—maybe a horse that he really loved to ride. Maybe some dogs. Maybe even his own saddle and bridle. I think the Willises had to sell almost everything they owned."

How would it be to suddenly lose everything? Kate tried to imagine it, but she couldn't. Still, she was sure that she wouldn't be as mean as Jimmy

Willis under the same circumstances!

She would show Jimmy, and she would show Mr. Willis, too. She was going to train Chinook, and she was going to ride him in Medicine Hat. And she was going to win!

CHAPTER
SIX

Mary Rides Brownie

Kate hadn't forgotten her promise to Mary Willis about Brownie. The next morning she found her old mare grazing in the meadow and tied her to the fence beside the barn. Then she walked over to the cabin for Mary.

Mary was helping Mrs. Willis weed the garden. As soon as she saw Kate, Mary jumped to her feet and waved. "Hi, Katie."

"Are you ready to ride Brownie?"

"You bet I am!" Mary replied.

Before Mrs. Willis finished pouring Kate a glass of ice tea, Mary had changed into her riding clothes: frontier pants, an old Western shirt, and a beat-up felt hat of Jimmy's.

"You look a sight!" Mary's mother said, laughing.

Mary was ready to ride. She wanted to run all the way back to the McGill barn—walking wasn't fast enough. And when Mary saw Brownie, she went right up to the mare and patted her neck.

"Mary, this is Brownie. Brownie, this is Mary," Kate said, introducing them.

"She's beautiful!" Mary said.

"Beautiful" wasn't exactly the word Kate would have used. Brownie was fat, swaybacked, and her forelock stuck straight out in front. But Brownie was a nice old mare with plenty of patience. The perfect horse for a beginning rider.

Mary said she already knew how to put a bridle on the horse. Kate helped her slide the bit into Brownie's mouth. Then Kate lifted Mary up so that she could slip the headstall over Brownie's ears.

Kate brought out her old saddle blanket, and the little saddle she had used when she first started riding. It would be a perfect fit for Mary.

Chinook was already saddled and waiting in his stall.

After they had led him over to where Brownie was standing, Kate asked Mary, "Would you like to ride out in the pasture?"

"Yes!" Mary said.

Kate gave Mary a leg up into the saddle. Brownie just twitched her ears and yawned. The rest of her didn't budge.

But once Kate had swung herself onto Chinook, the mare perked up. Kate and Mary set off up the trail to the cabin with Brutus and Stella right behind them.

Mary hadn't been able to ride much when her family had their own ranch. Jimmy had told Kate that most of the Willises' horses were young and barely broken, too wild for a child.

Mary was fearless.

Kate started Chinook out in a walk, but the pace wasn't quick enough for Mary.

"Let's go faster," she said.

Almost before the words were out of her mouth, Mary gave old Brownie a couple of kicks. They passed Kate and Chinook in a speedy trot. Mary bounced so hard in the saddle that Kate worried she might bite her tongue.

Kate nudged Chinook to catch up with them. And the two horses trotted all the way to the cabin and past it. Then the hills rose in front of them.

Kate was going to turn around and head back to the barn, but Mary asked, "Can we ride in there?" She pointed toward the hills.

Kate was about to say "no" when Chinook's ears suddenly pricked forward. Two large calves clattered past them.

"Oh, no!" Kate cried, "They must have broken through the fence, and now they're all running loose."

"What's the matter?" Mary asked, moving Brownie closer.

"I have to put these calves back where they belong," Kate told her. "Why don't you wait for me here? You can sit on that rock and let Brownie eat some grass."

"I can help!" Mary said.

"No, Mary, it's not safe. Stay here like I said."

Kate whistled for the dogs to run forward and nudged Chinook into a fast walk.

As the horse and dogs approached them, the calves stopped short. Their long ears swiveled back and forth while they tried to decide what to do.

Brutus and Stella began to bark. Chinook and Kate moved closer. The calves turned tail and galloped back towards the pen.

Kate swept up a third stray calf on her way in. She pushed all of the animals to the back of the pen. The three calves clumped together, peering out at the riders.

"Now you can help me, Mary. You and Brownie

stand right here in front of them, and don't let them move forward. I'll fix the fence."

Mary tugged on Brownie's reins until the mare stood squarely in front of the cattle. Brutus and Stella sat down beside them. The dogs' tongues hung out, but they were still on the job. All eyes were on the cattle.

Kate wrapped Chinook's reins around a bush. Then she checked the fence.

Two of the cross-pieces lay on the ground, splintered and broken. Kate dragged two logs from the wood pile and lifted them into place. She was about to close the fence when one of the bigger calves dashed past the little girl and Brownie.

Kate jumped on Chinook, and they were off in a flash after the runaway calf. Kate and Chinook cut the calf off in no time, and returned him to the pen.

Mary clapped loudly. "You were great, Kate!"

"Hey! What are you doing?" a voice demanded loudly.

Kate looked over her shoulder and saw Jimmy Willis running towards them.

"Why is Mary here?" Jimmy asked Kate.

"I'm teaching her to ride," Kate answered. "Not that it's any of your business."

"If it concerns my sister, it's my business," Jimmy

shot back. He turned to Mary. "Does Ma know you're here?"

Mary nodded.

"So you girls are playing at being cowboys?" he asked. His lips twitched, and Kate could tell he was amused.

"We're not playing at anything. Some calves broke loose from the pen, and I rounded them up." Kate's eyes flashed.

"And I helped," Mary piped up. "I watched the calves while Kate fixed the fence."

Jimmy walked over to the fence and inspected it. "Not a bad job," he said grudgingly.

"Thanks." Kate grinned.

"For a girl."

Kate turned away. She was tired of being insulted by Jimmy Willis. "Come on, Mary. Let's ride back." Kate flicked Chinook's reins and headed down the trail. When she'd gone several feet, she stopped. She looked over her shoulder and called out, "Jimmy Willis, you're stubborn as a mule when it comes to girls, but I'm going to change your mind. Just wait and see."

Mabel the Milk Cow

Early each morning, Kate was busy with her own chores, and with Brian's, too. While Brian rode over to the Frasers' ranch to throw a baseball around, Kate fed the chickens and gathered the eggs. She fed and milked the McGills' dairy cow, Mabel. Then she fed Chinook, groomed him, and cleaned out his box stall.

When Kate was finished with all that, she saddled up her horse and reined him in the corral near the barn. They did figure eights, circles, rollbacks, and spins until Kate's head was ready to spin.

They were practicing sliding stops one morning a few days after her birthday when Mr. McGill called to her over the fence.

"Joe, Jimmy, Peter, and I are riding out to the back pasture to take a look at the cows and calves there," Mr. McGill said. The back pasture was several miles away from the ranch house. "Want to come?"

Any other time, Kate would have jumped at the offer. But as soon as Mr. McGill said that the others were going, Kate's only thought was, "Now's my chance to start training Chinook!"

It would take the men all day to ride out to the back pasture, look at all of the cows there, and ride back again. Mrs. McGill had probably packed a lunch for them, too. Which meant that Kate would have hours to put her own plans into action.

So Kate answered, "No, thanks, Dad. I think I'll work with Chinook some more."

She hung around the barn while her dad, Peter, Mr. Willis, and Jimmy saddled up their horses. Peter rode Peppy—it was important to keep his cutting horse exercised. Mr. McGill rode his favorite horse, a big bay named Charlie. Mr. Willis rode Star, a young chestnut mare. And Jimmy rode a black horse named Thunder. When he swung into the saddle, Kate saw Jimmy smile for the first time. And she knew Jimmy *did* love to ride, probably just as much as she did.

Once the four of them had headed up the trail toward the back pasture, with Brutus and Stella tagging behind, Kate got busy.

First, she went into the house to tell her mother: "Mom, I'm going to ride out toward the cabin."

"That's fine, honey," said Mrs. McGill. "Say hello to Cora Willis for me."

"I will if I see her," said Kate, hoping that she wouldn't see anyone. "Could I take a lunch with me, like Dad and the others?" she asked her mom.

"I've got an extra roast-beef sandwich," her mother said. "I'll wrap it in waxed paper."

Kate slipped the sandwich into the pocket of her jacket. She was set for the rest of the day. Now for the important part of her plan: getting Mabel the milk cow to the box canyon.

In the hills behind the old cabin, there was a small box canyon. In it, Kate's grandfather had built a corral for his horses. It was hidden away from prying eyes, so it would be perfect for training Chinook.

Kate found Mabel chewing her cud near the stock tank. Mabel was not at all happy about leaving the barn. But with a lot of pushing from Kate and Chinook, she finally ambled away in the direction of the cabin.

Kate made sure that Chinook moved Mabel along the trail at a slow and easy pace. By the time they were halfway to the cabin, she was more certain than ever that Chinook was going to be a wonderful cutting horse.

He kept his ears pricked straight forward, fixed on Mabel. His eyes never left the cow, either. If Mabel took a step or two to either side of the trail, Chinook did the same to bring her back in line. It was almost as though he could read Mabel's mind!

"Cow smarts," Kate said to Chinook, patting his neck. "You've definitely got them!"

As they neared the cabin, Kate crossed her fingers in the hope that Mrs. Willis and the younger children would be indoors. Grandpa McGill had planted a thick row of pine trees along the sides and back of the cabin as a windbreak. If Kate and Chinook—and Mabel—could reach the pines without being seen, they were home free.

Suddenly a small voice called, "Kate? Katie!" It was Mary Willis, standing on the front porch of the cabin with her little brother in her arms.

"What are you doing, Katie?" Mary called to her. "May I ride on your horse with you?"

"I'm just rounding up the milk cow," Kate called back, waving to Mary. "I'd better hurry." She felt a little guilty. She'd make it up to Mary by giving her another riding lesson soon.

Kate gave Chinook a nudge. He pushed Mabel into

a trot. They moved behind the trees and into the hills before anyone else saw them.

Kate guided Chinook and the cow down a dry stream bed and into a small box canyon with a flowing spring at the back. Steep slopes formed three sides of the little canyon. The entrance could be closed off by adding two more crosspieces to a split rail fence. The whole thing wasn't much bigger than the cutting pen in Medicine Hat, and it was totally private.

Now Kate was ready to train a cutting horse!

There was plenty for her to keep in mind. For one thing, she had to remember how to use the reins with both hands to direct Chinook by pulling on one rein and pushing against his neck with the other. She also had to think about what she did with her legs. If she pressed with her right leg, Chinook would move to the left. If she pressed with her left, he would move to the right. Pressing both legs would move him forward.

And Kate always had to remember to sit straight up, in the middle of the saddle. If she leaned forward, or to one side, she could throw Chinook off balance. If she wanted to stop him, though, she should lean her body back, and push herself down in the saddle.

In a real cutting-horse contest, there would be a whole herd of cows to choose from. Choosing a cow that could be worked well was part of the contest. But Mr. McGill felt that a new horse should start with just one cow.

"We've got our cow—now we'll see what we can do with her," Kate said, giving Chinook's neck a pat.

By now, Mabel had moved into the shade of a hill, and she was chewing her cud again. The cow's eyes were half closed. She didn't bother to open them any wider as Kate and Chinook walked toward her. But Chinook was looking hard at the cow, showing what Kate's dad called "cow interest."

When they got closer—about ten or twelve feet away from Mabel—the cow finally opened her eyes. And she shifted her feet a little. Without any directions from Kate, Chinook followed Mabel's movements with his head. Mabel took a couple of steps to the right . . . and Kate nudged Chinook with her left foot to do the same.

Mabel stopped. Kate stopped Chinook by sitting back in the saddle. With both hands on the reins, she made sure that Chinook was facing Mabel squarely. She nudged him toward the cow again, just far enough to make her move a little.

Mabel moved farther to the right. Chinook moved with her. Mabel stopped. Chinook stopped.

Kate nudged her horse a step or two closer. This

time Mabel doubled back to the left. Chinook's head followed her, and Kate directed the rest of his body to do the same.

She had heard her dad tell Peter a hundred times, "You want Peppy to stop, then to turn, and always to control the cow."

Kate let Mabel circle the whole canyon once, with Chinook keeping pace—that was called "tracking" the cow. Then Kate had Chinook move forward enough to stop Mabel. Chinook stopped, too. When Mabel turned in the opposite direction, Chinook moved with her.

"Good boy!" said Kate proudly.

Kate hadn't had to tell him to do it. Chinook was already moving with the cow, on his own.

Paying such close attention was hard work for Chinook. Even though it was cool in the canyon, Kate could see that her horse was beginning to breathe faster.

"If your horse starts breathing hard . . . STOP!" Mr. McGill always said. "Never let him run out of air, or he'll end up getting hurt."

Mabel was looking a little tired, too. A tired cow might not give any milk, which Kate *sure* didn't want.

She waited until Mabel stopped again, and Chinook stopped with her. Then Kate tightened up on the reins and pulled Chinook off the cow, turning him

away from Mabel to show him that the contest was over.

She let Chinook and Mabel rest in the shade for a while as she ate her lunch. Then she started working with them again.

About the middle of the afternoon, Kate had some unexpected visitors. She was concentrating so hard that she didn't notice Jimmy Willis until it was too late.

"Hey, what are you doing back here?" a voice demanded suddenly.

Kate glanced around to see Jimmy on Thunder on the far side of the fence, along with Brutus and Stella. The dogs were wagging their tails happily. They had picked up Kate's trail at the barn and led Jimmy straight to her.

"Traitors!" Kate murmured under her breath about the dogs. Then, louder, she answered Jimmy: "I'm not doing anything—just fooling around."

"You're cutting on Chinook," Jimmy Willis said. "Or pretending to."

"It's not pretending!" Kate said hotly, too angry to worry about Jimmy telling on her.

"Whatever it is, it's bothering the milk cow," Jimmy said. "And your dad sent me to bring her back home." He paused for a second, then added, "Besides, girls can't cut. Everybody knows that."

"I can cut better than you ever dreamed of cutting!" Kate said, furious.

"I don't think so," said Jimmy. "I'll bet I can ride Chinook better than you can."

"You can't, and I'll prove it," said Kate. "The first chance we get, we'll come back here. Each of us will ride Chinook to cut a cow."

"Why would I want to do that?" Jimmy said, sounding as if he were above it all.

"I'll tell you why! Because—if you're better," said Kate, "then you can ride him in Medicine Hat at the fair. If I'm better . . ."

"You won't be," said Jimmy quickly.

Now he sounded interested. As far as Jimmy was concerned, he had already beaten her.

"If I'm better, then I'll ride him at the fair," Kate finished.

"You're a girl! You can't ride him in Medicine Hat, no matter who wins here," Jimmy pointed out.

"If I win . . . you'll help me do it somehow!" Kate said. "Is it a deal?"

But Jimmy had thought of something else. "Who decides who's better?" he asked her.

"We'll go by the rules of the contest, and we'll both decide who wins," said Kate. "Is it a deal?"

"It's a deal," said Jimmy. "Now—I have to get this cow back to the barn."

Brian and Peppy

As soon as Jimmy Willis rode away from the canyon with Mabel, Kate began to worry, just a little. What if—by a stroke of bad luck—Jimmy rode Chinook better than she did the day of their contest? And what if it were Jimmy, not Kate, who ended up winning a prize on Chinook in Medicine Hat?

She didn't even want to think about it!

At breakfast the next morning, she was glad to hear her dad announce, "Brian, you and Peter and I have to get busy on Peppy." Kate hoped to pick up some useful tips on cutting before her contest with Jimmy.

Brian wasn't glad, however. "But Asa's coming

60

over any minute . . . ," he began.

"Asa will just have to wait," said his father. "You and Peppy have to get used to each other if you want to do well in Medicine Hat. And I think we should get started now, before Peter leaves for college." Their trip to Edmonton was only two days away.

"All right, Dad," Brian mumbled. "I'll ride Peppy."

Kate had her chores to do. But she took time out to watch Brian warming up the gray horse in the corral.

Peppy was a little taller than Chinook, and heavier. He had a larger head, and he carried it lower. Peppy was a beautiful steel-gray color, with a light gray-and-cream mane and tail. Kate thought that Chinook was a prettier horse, and that he moved better. On the other hand, Peppy was five years older than Chinook, with five years of cutting-horse competitions behind him.

Peppy and Peter were a real team. But Peppy behaved differently with Brian than he did with Peter—Kate could see that right away. With Peter, Peppy moved freely and smoothly. Peter barely had to nudge Peppy to get him to break into a long, easy lope.

But as Brian reined the horse in figure eights and circles, Peppy's lope got slower and choppier. Soon he was trotting—and Peppy's trot was rough.

"I hate doing this!" Brian said to Kate as he circled the corral. "And Peppy knows it."

"But don't you want to place in the cutting this August?" Kate asked him.

"I don't want to go at all," said Brian. "And I'm sure not going to win anything, not with Peppy acting up and all of those people staring at me."

"I can't think of anything I'd rather do," said Kate.

"And I wish you could!" said her twin. "You're better on Peppy than I am, and that stuff about no girls is stupid."

Kate thought of telling him about her plan for Chinook. But she didn't. What if Jimmy Willis ended up riding her horse?

Mr. McGill and Peter penned some cattle from the home pasture for Peppy to work with—six big calves and three cows. And Mr. McGill turned back for Brian on his bay horse, Charlie. A turn-back man keeps the cow or calf that a cutter is working from running too far away.

Kate never left the corral fence, because she wanted to hear every word Mr. McGill and Peter said. It was the next best thing to having them work with her and Chinook.

"Let Peppy turn with his nose first," Mr. McGill would say to Brian. "And don't pull on him—the rest of his body will follow his nose."

Which was good advice for Kate and Chinook, too.

Or Peter might say, "Don't let him make any false moves. Force the cow to move first by pushing Peppy toward her. Then Peppy will move *with* her."

Or Mr. McGill: "Don't go so fast, Brian. You can slow Peppy down and still handle a cow. In fact, you will handle the cow better."

Kate nodded from her perch on the fence. In the canyon, sometimes Chinook had gotten so excited about what he was doing that he tried to move Mabel—and himself—much too quickly. Now Kate could see how much easier it would be if she made Chinook take things more slowly.

Peter also said, "Be sure that your horse is always facing the cow, Brian, even if you have to pull back on the reins. And always make a clean stop before you turn."

Perhaps the most important advice Mr. McGill gave Brian was: "Study the cattle, and take your time making a cut. You need a cow that moves well, so you can get a good performance out of your horse. Remember—you only have two-and-a-half minutes to show what you can do."

Kate was learning a lot.

But for Brian, having to practice on Peppy meant

taking time out from what he'd much rather be doing: playing baseball. Asa Fraser rode his horse over in time for lunch. He and Brian talked about baseball the whole time, while Kate thought about Chinook and her upcoming contest with Jimmy Willis.

That afternoon, she just rode her horse in the corral. And the next day, she didn't get to ride Chinook at all. After chores, she helped her mother fix a huge farewell dinner for Peter: beef ribs cooked on a campfire outside, a big pot of baked beans, pickled tomatoes, summer squash, and Peter's favorite dessert—a giant German chocolate cake, with lots of canned coconut.

The Willises were invited, and Brian had asked Asa Fraser to come, too, and spend the night.

The grown-ups talked to each other.

Brian and Asa talked about baseball, of course.

Jimmy didn't say a word until just before the Willises left that night. Then he had a chance to speak to Kate alone.

"My dad's going to be exercising your brother's horse the day after tomorrow," Jimmy said in a low voice. "Your father asked him to ride Peppy along the fence-line of the home pasture." He went on, "That's miles of barbed-wire to check for breaks—my dad will be busy for hours. So I'll meet you as soon as I've done my chores, and we'll go to the canyon."

Kate's stomach lurched—their contest would happen so soon? But she whispered back, "I'll have Thunder saddled."

Then she noticed that Brian and Asa were watching them. After the Willises had left, Brian asked Kate, "What did he want? He wasn't being rude to you, was he?"

"Jimmy Willis only opens his mouth when he has something mean to say," Asa agreed.

Kate didn't want to lie to them. But she didn't want to tell them about her plans for Chinook, either— at least, not yet. So all she could come up with was, "Sometimes Jimmy's not so bad."

"You could have fooled me!" said Brian, frowning.

Kate knew exactly how Brian felt, since Jimmy hadn't really done anything to change her mind about him.

Mr. McGill walked over to them then. "We have a big day tomorrow," he said. "We'd better get to bed."

Kate was sure that Brian and Asa would stay up half the night, jabbering about the baseball game that Brian would be seeing in Edmonton. But she fell asleep as soon as her head hit the pillow.

In what seemed like no time at all, her mother opened her bedroom door and said, "Wake up, Katie.

Breakfast is ready. Don't let it get cold."

Brian and Asa looked bleary-eyed. And Peter looked excited, a little nervous, and sad, all at once.

Mrs. McGill mostly looked sad. And proud, of course. "You're the first in the family to go to college," she said to her oldest son. "And that's wonderful. But that won't keep me from missing you."

"I'll write all the time, Mom," Peter promised. "And I'll be home for the holidays."

"Maybe we'll visit him in Edmonton, too, Emma," Mr. McGill said, his arm around her. "It will be fine." But Mr. McGill looked almost as sad as his wife.

Brian and Asa helped Peter load his trunk and boxes onto the wagon behind the Model T. In one of those boxes was a hooked rug Mrs. McGill had made for him. "So you won't have to step out of bed onto a cold floor," she told Peter.

Mrs. McGill had packed a lunch for them, too.

Soon it was time to go. Kate, Brian, and Peter climbed into the back seat of the Model T, their parents into the front.

Asa waved good-bye one last time. "Write down everything that happens at the baseball game, so you won't forget!" he called to Brian.

Then they were bumping down the dirt road that led to the train. As they passed the cabin, Mrs. Willis and Mary waved from the porch.

"I don't see Jimmy anywhere," Kate's mom said.

"Joe keeps him busy," said her dad.

The dirt road took them past the one-room schoolhouse where the McGills went to school, along with the children from the other ranches in the district: Asa and his little brother, Angus; the three Metcalfe girls; Roberta and David Johnston; and the Robbs.

Peter must have been thinking about their neighbors because he said, "Brian, see to it that you beat Justin Robb in Medicine Hat."

Justin's older brother, Richard, and Peter had been competing against each other in the cutting for years. Peter and Peppy usually did better than Richard and the Robbs' tall black horse, Skyrocket. Now Richard would be going away to college, too. But Justin Robb would be riding in Medicine Hat. Justin was the same age as Brian and Kate.

"You need to keep up the family tradition, son," Mr. McGill added.

"Yes, sir," was all Brian said. But Kate saw him sigh as he gazed out the window of the Model T.

Kate would love to beat the pants off Justin Robb, who bragged too much, anyway. And maybe she would!

The train was waiting for them when they drove up to the railhead, the last stop for this branch of the Canadian Pacific Railway. There was no station, or anything like a building. The tracks just ended in the tall grass of the prairie.

Clouds of gray smoke were billowing from the smokestack. And Mr. Coulter, the engineer, leaned out of the locomotive to call, "How far are you going this time, Mr. McGill?"

"My sons and I are going all the way to Edmonton!" Mr. McGill called back.

Mr. Coulter nodded. "All abo-o-oard!" he said. The train always left at 10:20 A.M., on the dot.

There was just enough time for Kate and her mother to give Peter one last hug. Mr. McGill loaded Peter's trunk and boxes, and a suitcase for him and Brian, into the boxcar.

"Have a good year, son. And work hard. But not too hard," Mrs. McGill said to Peter, with tears in her eyes.

"I will. And I won't," Peter said, grinning at her. "And thanks for the rug, Mom."

Brian had already run up the steps of the passenger car. He was pushing open one of the windows. "You'd better hurry," he yelled to his brother and father. "Because I'm not missing the ball game.

Not even if I have to go to Edmonton all by myself!"

Mr. McGill hugged his wife. Mrs. McGill kissed Peter good-bye. Mr. Coulter tooted the train whistle, fired up the engine . . . and the McGill men swung themselves onto the platform of the passenger car and stepped inside.

Everybody waved.

Then they were gone, heading down the track in the direction of Medicine Hat, then Calgary, and hundreds of miles later, Edmonton.

CHAPTER
NINE

Contest in the Canyon

Early the next morning, Kate saw Mr. Willis
saddling Peppy. He tipped his hat to her as he started
the gray horse up the fence line in a brisk trot.

Kate quickly finished her chores. She was just
saddling Jimmy's horse, Thunder, when Jimmy raced
up to her.

"I trapped some young steers in the canyon early
this morning," he said, out of breath.

"Young steers?" Kate repeated anxiously. She had
only worked Chinook on old Mabel. She had no idea
how he would act around several friskier animals.

"Three steers and a cow. They'll move better than
Mabel, and give us more of a chance to show what we

can do," Jimmy Willis said cockily. He seemed awfully sure of himself. "Let's get Thunder and Chinook saddled up," he added. "If we hurry, we'll be back in time for lunch, without anybody missing us."

It was about a mile and a half to the box canyon. The two horses covered the distance quickly in an easy lope.

It was the first time that Kate had actually ridden with Jimmy. She could see what an excellent rider he was, easy and relaxed, his hands gentle on the reins. And it didn't make her feel any better.

"You're good on a horse," Kate said, her heart sinking.

"I've learned a lot from my dad," Jimmy said. "He's one of the best cowboys around."

Maybe he read something in Kate's face, because he added quickly, "We didn't lose our ranch because we were bad ranchers. We lost it because we had bad luck."

When they reached the box canyon, Chinook nickered excitedly at the sight of the cattle Jimmy had penned. The four young animals had been grazing. Now they raised their heads in the air, staring warily at the riders. As Kate and Jimmy rode closer to the fence, they trotted toward the back wall of the canyon.

"We'll each cut twice, all right?" Jimmy said to

Kate. "Go ahead—I'll take the fence down for you." He slipped off of Thunder to remove two of the fence rails.

Kate didn't want to go first! She wanted Jimmy to ride before she did, so that she could watch him and see how well she would have to do to beat him.

But Jimmy probably had the same thoughts. "Ladies first," he insisted with a grin, waving her through the fence.

Kate squared her shoulders and nudged Chinook forward. "I might as well get it over with," she told herself.

She and Chinook moved quietly closer to the cattle. The animals bunched tightly together and turned to face them, their backs to a wall of the canyon.

As far as Kate knew, it was Chinook's first time to walk into a herd of cattle and cut one out. The horse was excited and a little nervous—Kate could feel his tension as he gazed first at one big calf, and then another.

In a real cutting contest, Kate wouldn't have been allowed to help Chinook by pulling on the reins. But now he was still learning. So Kate guided him toward the cow by pulling on the left rein.

Both the cow and one of the steers started

walking away from the herd to the left. The steer's body was between the older cow and Chinook. Kate urged Chinook forward, aiming him at the steer's shoulder. The steer stopped dead.

The cow, on the far side, kept moving to the left. Kate nudged Chinook toward the cow's hip, to push her even farther out of the herd.

Now they had her. The cow was standing about eight feet away from the rest of the herd. Kate quickly moved Chinook into the gap, pushing the cow even farther away from the other cattle, into the middle of the canyon.

"We're really doing it!" Kate murmured. The match had begun. Chinook had been watching the cow closely since Kate had first nudged him toward her. As soon as the cow tried to get back into the herd, the horse lowered his head and stepped in the same direction. The cow stopped, facing Chinook. Chinook stopped, too. The cow suddenly dodged to the right, hoping to get around Chinook. But Chinook dodged to the right as well. The cow stopped again, and so did the horse.

Then the cow dashed to the left! Kate thought Chinook was going to lose her. But he whirled to the left himself. He moved so quickly that Kate had to hang on to the saddle horn to keep from falling off.

But Chinook didn't lose the cow. The cow stopped again, facing him.

"You're already better at this than I am!" Kate said out loud to her horse.

Jimmy Willis laughed. But for the first time Kate didn't feel that he was laughing *at* her. "Good move!" he called out.

Kate turned Chinook away from the cow, so he would know that they were finished with her—that was what cutters calling "quitting the cow."

The cow ran back into the herd, and Kate chose a black steer to work next.

But she and Chinook didn't do as well with their steer. He was wild, and he was fast, too. Chinook was hot and jumpy, and Kate was anxious, and together they made mistakes.

Twice, Chinook turned too far to one side, losing a clear view of the black steer. One of those times, the steer got back into the herd.

In a real cutting contest, that meant points off. Kate just hoped it wasn't going to make the difference between *her* going to Medicine Hat and Jimmy Willis going. Before Jimmy took his turn on Chinook, he and Kate sat for a while to let the horse cool down.

"Chinook will be a champion," Jimmy said. "He's already good, and he's going to be great." He was quiet for a second. Then he went on, "So how are we going to work this out? If I do better today . . ."

If Jimmy Willis did better, competing in Medicine Hat wouldn't be a problem for him. "I'd just tell Dad that I wanted you to ride Chinook in the first-timers' class—and that would be that," Kate said.

But she didn't want Jimmy to ride Chinook. He was *her* horse, and she wanted to ride him at the fair!

"What if I do better?" Kate asked Jimmy.

"If you do better . . ." Jimmy frowned as though he hadn't seriously considered that. After a moment he continued, "You could stick your hair up under a cowboy hat. And sign up in Medicine Hat using a boy's name . . ."

"But how would I get to the fair?" Kate wondered. It would take much too long to ride there—a day and a night, probably. And the train was out: Peppy rode to Medicine Hat on the train, which meant that Chinook couldn't, not in secret.

"Let's worry about that when it happens. If it happens," Jimmy said. "I think it's my turn now."

He picked the friskiest steer in the herd to work with—a red one with a white face. While Kate held her breath, Jimmy and Chinook moved the steer out of the herd.

At first, everything went right. The horse moved

with the steer as if they were linked together. But Jimmy pressed Chinook too hard. Instead of slowing the horse, and the steer, down—Kate remembered her dad's advice to Brian—Jimmy kept nudging Chinook with his legs.

And Jimmy didn't know about making the horse come to a full stop before turning, either. So Chinook was scrambling through his turns, out of balance. Jimmy and Chinook lost the red steer—he raced back into the herd.

Then Jimmy chose the black steer that Kate and Chinook had already worked. Maybe Jimmy thought he would have a better chance with the animal, because he'd seen what the steer was likely to do.

But by then Chinook was too keyed up to pay close attention. The horse made a few false moves, trying to guess what the steer might do. And Jimmy was still pushing him too hard. They lost the black steer, too.

It was over. Jimmy had let two steers get away. Kate had only lost one. So Kate had clearly won!

Jimmy rode Chinook slowly back to the fence where Kate was waiting. She knew she had a relieved smile on her face—she couldn't help herself.

"You won fair and square," Jimmy said to her, climbing down from the saddle. "I'm a good rider. So are you. But you know a lot more about cutting than I do."

He wasn't going to be a sore loser.

"Thanks," Kate said, taking Chinook's reins from him. "Are you still going to help me?" she asked.

"I gave my word," Jimmy said. "And I'll keep it. You'll ride Chinook in Medicine Hat this summer . . . somehow."

Brian's False Step

As they rode up to the barn that afternoon, Jimmy muttered, "Uh-oh—my dad's back!"

Mr. Willis was grooming Peppy near the corral. When he saw Jimmy and Kate, he didn't seem pleased. "Good afternoon," he said politely to Kate, before asking his son, "Jim, just where have you been? I looked all over for you—and I could have used some help fixing a break in the fence."

Kate's heart stopped. She could imagine Jimmy answering, "Kate and I were cutting on Chinook in the box canyon."

Jimmy didn't say anything at all for a few seconds. Then he murmured, "I'm sorry, Dad. I promise you that

79

it won't happen again."

"Go unsaddle your horse," Mr. Willis told him. "Walk him around, then wipe him down, and brush him really well. And see to it that he gets some water."

"Yes, sir," Jimmy said. He turned Thunder toward the barn door, with Kate following.

"Thanks for not telling on me," Kate whispered as they pulled their saddles off inside the barn. "And I'm sorry your father's angry."

"He'll get over it," Jimmy said, gathering up the grooming brushes.

"Still . . . thanks anyway," Kate repeated. Now she had learned something else about Jimmy—he could keep a secret.

For the next few days, Mr. Willis kept Jimmy busy— too busy to help Kate with Chinook. She worked her horse on the steers in the box canyon by herself. Then Mr. McGill and Brian came back from Edmonton.

Brian was barely off the train at the railhead when he started in about baseball. "It was incredible!" Brian said to his twin. "We saw two games. In the first one, the Rangers shut out the Hawks: the final score was 9 to 0!"

"'Shut out?'" said Kate.

"It means one team keeps the other team from scoring," said Brian, climbing into the Model T. "In the second game, Bob McElway—he's the Rangers' pitcher—hit a home run! The ball flew so far up in the air I almost couldn't see it, and then it sailed all the way over the left field wall! The Rangers won, 4 to 1!"

"But what about Peter?" Mrs. McGill interrupted before Brian could give a rundown of each of the Rangers players. "What did his college room look like? Was he all right when you left him?"

"And Edmonton?" Kate asked, prodding Brian to get his mind off baseball for a second. "Did you like the hotel?"

"It was fine. I liked the trolley cars," said Brian, before he launched into more facts about the Rangers: "Bruce Culver, the Rangers' catcher, is amazing! He can . . ."

Mrs. McGill started laughing. "Kate, maybe we'll have to get our questions answered by your father."

As they bumped toward the ranch in the car, Mr. McGill told them about Peter's college in Edmonton: "All of the buildings are made of brick and stone. There's a big library, and a playing field. Peter's room is small, but he has a window overlooking a park with trees and flowers. When we left, he'd already met two boys on his floor. He's fine, Emma," Mr. McGill said.

Then Mr. McGill asked them, "How did everything go at the ranch while we were away? Did you find the time to ride Chinook, Kate?"

Mrs. McGill answered for her: "She rode him every day. Sometimes I didn't see Kate from morning till late afternoon."

"Good for you, Katie," said Mr. McGill. "First thing tomorrow we'll get back to work, too, won't we, Brian? We paid Peppy's entry fees when we stopped at Medicine Hat," he told Kate and Mrs. McGill.

Now that her father was back, it was harder than ever for Kate to sneak off to the canyon to work Chinook on cattle. But she did rein her horse in the big corral when Brian wasn't riding Peppy there.

Brian and Peppy weren't getting along any better in cutting practice. Peppy was a smart horse—he could tell when Brian's mind was on other things, like home runs, or pitching a no-hitter, instead of cattle. And if Brian didn't care about what was going on in the corral, then Peppy wasn't going to care, either.

The gray horse would take the bit in his teeth and pay no attention to Brian's hands on the reins. He would turn with his shoulder first, instead of with his nose. Then he started slowing down enough to let calves slip past him.

Once Brian even lost his seat on Peppy.

During their practice, a calf raced to the left. Then it whirled to the right. Brian wasn't sitting straight in the saddle, and Peppy could feel it. Instead of moving smoothly with the calf, Peppy came dow'. hard on his front feet . . . Brian sailed out of the saddle and landed in the dirt!

Brian scrambled to his feet and scowled at the horse, his face red with embarrassment.

"The last thing we need is for you to get hurt—or for Peppy to get hurt—and miss the contest in Medicine Hat altogether," Mr. McGill said sternly. "Try again, son."

But Peppy didn't cause Brian any more problems. Something completely unexpected did.

Asa had come over to the McGill ranch after lunch one day. He and Brian were behind the barn with their ball and bat, pretending to be players on the Edmonton teams: Brian was a Ranger, and Asa a Hawk.

Kate and Jimmy Willis were grooming Chinook near the stock tank. They could see the ballplayers, and hear Brian talking as if he were announcing a baseball game through a loudspeaker: "Bruce Harris of the Hawks is stepping up to the plate . . . Bob McElway, the Rangers' pitcher, is winding up . . . he's throwing . . . Harris swings. He hits! It's a fly ball . . ."

Brian was announcing and running backward at the same time. He held his glove up in the air over his head. His eyes were squinting into the sun, trying to spot the soaring ball.

Brian must have stepped in a hole, because Kate and Jimmy suddenly saw him fall, and heard him cry out in pain.

Asa called to him, "Brian? You okay?"

Brian didn't answer.

Kate and Jimmy Willis stopped brushing Chinook and glanced at each other. "Are you all right?" Kate yelled to her brother.

"I . . . I don't think so . . . ," Brian replied in a strained voice.

Kate dropped her brush and sprinted toward him.

"Mrs. McGill? Mrs. McGill—help!" Asa was shouting. Kate's mother ran down the front steps of the ranch house and over to the barn.

Brian was sitting on the ground. His left leg was tucked under him. His right leg was stretched out in front. He was holding onto it with both hands and staring down at his ankle.

"What happened, honey?" said Mrs. McGill, kneeling beside Brian.

Brian's face was very white. "I . . . guess I . . . tripped," he said to his mother. "I think I sprained my ankle . . ."

Kate didn't know much about medicine. But the

ankle looked more than sprained to her.

It was swelling up, like a sprained ankle. But it was also bent at a funny angle. Kate thought maybe Brian's ankle was broken!

Her mother must have been thinking the same thing.

"Don't move, Brian," Mrs. McGill said. "We'll get your dad." She turned to Kate and said, "The men are on the tractor about half a mile down the south fence—go get your father, right away."

Jimmy Willis was leading Chinook into the barn when Kate ran back to him.

"Brian's hurt—I have to find my father," Kate said.

"I'll saddle Chinook," said Jimmy.

"There isn't time," said Kate. "I'll ride him bareback."

Jimmy led the horse to the corral, so that Kate could climb the fence and slide onto Chinook's broad back.

When she galloped away, Kate was riding Chinook bareback, with only a halter rope for reins.

Chinook flew down the south fence-line. Kate could feel the muscles moving in her horse's strong back. Chinook's skin was warm against her legs. If Kate hadn't been frightened for Brian, she would have been having a wonderful ride.

Mr. McGill frowned when he saw Kate pulling Chinook to a sliding stop beside him.

"Katie, you may feel that you can trust your horse enough to ride him bareback," Mr. McGill said. "But what if he saw something that spooked him? It's possible he could . . ."

Kate interrupted him. "Dad, Brian's hurt. It's his ankle. And Mom wants you, right away!" she said.

"I'll take your horse," Mr. McGill said.

Kate slid down, off Chinook, and her father swung himself up on the horse. The two of them were gone in a cloud of dust, heading back to the ranch house.

"I'll give you a ride back on the tractor," Mr. Willis said to Kate.

The tractor was much slower than Chinook. By the time Kate and Joe Willis got to the ranch house, Mr. McGill was carrying Brian to the Model T. Mrs. McGill was following with a pillow. Asa Fraser and Jimmy stood back, out of the way. Jimmy was holding a sweaty Chinook by his halter rope.

While Mrs. McGill got Brian settled in the back seat of the car, Mr. McGill spotted Kate and Joe Willis.

"Katie, we're driving your brother into Medicine Hat so that Dr. Hall can take a look at his ankle," Mr. McGill said. "I want you to go over to the Willises, and stay with them until we get back. Okay with you, Joe?"

Mr. Willis nodded. "Glad to have her," he said. "If you need to stay in Medicine Hat overnight, Kate can bunk with Mary."

"Thanks, Joe," Mr. McGill said.

When he leaned down to give Kate a quick kiss on the cheek, she asked in a low voice, "Do you think Brian's ankle is broken, Dad?"

"I'm afraid it might be," said Mr. McGill.

He climbed into the car and started the engine. "We'll get back here as soon as we can," Mr. McGill said.

Mrs. McGill waved good-bye as the Model T pulled onto the dirt road. Brian's pale face stared out the back window.

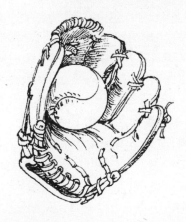

The Plan

As soon as Asa Fraser had saddled his horse and left for home, Jimmy said, "I'm sorry your brother hurt himself. But he sure won't be riding in Medicine Hat. Even if his ankle is just sprained, he only has two weeks until the cutting-horse contest. So what if you borrowed some of his clothes, and . . ."

"Jimmy Willis!" Kate said angrily. "How can you even think about that right now?"

But at the same time, a small voice in her own head had been saying, "Here's your chance to compete in the cutting in Medicine Hat: you can ride into the arena as Brian McGill. The entry fees are paid—Dad said so. A McGill horse has a stall waiting for him there, at the horse barn. Why shouldn't Chinook get the stall now?"

Jimmy muttered, "Forget it!" He turned his back on Kate and led Chinook toward the barn.

Jimmy and his dad took the tractor down the south fence that afternoon, so Kate didn't see him until evening. Back at the cabin for dinner, Kate told him she was sorry for snapping at him earlier.

"I had been thinking the same thing," she admitted. "Now that Brian is hurt, maybe there was a way I could ride Chinook in Medicine Hat. And I felt terrible for thinking it."

"You didn't make it happen," Jimmy pointed out. "And Brian would want you to compete, if he can't."

"You think so?" said Kate, hoping he was right.

Jimmy nodded. "Now all we have to figure out is how to get you there."

Kate thought again of the train, now that Brian probably wouldn't be competing. But if Brian didn't compete, maybe nobody would be going to the fair. And how could she and Jimmy sneak away to Medicine Hat without anyone noticing?

The McGills brought Brian back from Medicine Hat the next morning. Kate's brother looked a little better—his face wasn't as pale as the day before. But his right leg was encased in a plaster cast to the knee.

Mr. McGill carried Brian into the house. Mrs. McGill followed with two brand-new crutches for him to use.

"My ankle's really broken," Brian said to Kate while they settled him in the spare room downstairs.

"But not too badly," said Mrs. McGill, plumping up his pillows. "Dr. Hall said it's more of a crack than a big break."

"He said I can't play baseball for six weeks!" Brian groaned.

"Dr. Hall said your cast will be on for six weeks," his mother told him. "No baseball for two months, at least."

"And definitely no riding, either," Kate was thinking. And her dad echoed her thoughts when he said sadly, "There won't be a McGill in the cutting-horse contest this year."

"Alan, don't make the boy feel bad," Mrs. McGill said to her husband.

Kate thought Brian had looked much more upset about missing two months of baseball practice than about giving up the fair! "Anyway," she said to herself, "there might be a McGill in the cutting, after all."

What her father said next made everything seem easier. "We'll watch the cutting in Medicine Hat, anyway," he told Kate. "Adults cut on a Thursday morning, under eighteen's in the afternoon. You and Joe Willis and I will drive in for the day while your mother stays here and keeps Brian company."

"That's great, Dad!" Kate said, her heart suddenly pounding. She was going to Medicine Hat with her dad, and Joe Willis was going to be there, too, instead of keeping Jimmy busy at the ranch. So Chinook could go to Medicine Hat on the train, if Jimmy was willing to take him. She couldn't wait to tell Jimmy!

The night before the contest, Kate stashed a pair of her brother's riding pants, one of his hats, and a leather belt with "Brian" stamped on it into the back of the Model T.

Mr. McGill, Joe Willis, and Kate would be leaving in the Model T at sunup the next day. No one would be likely to see Jimmy saddle up Chinook and set off up the dirt road to the railhead. Kate had already given him five of her ten silver dollars—birthday presents from her Aunt May and Uncle Randy—to pay the fare to Medicine Hat for himself and her horse.

The train left the railhead at 10:20 A.M., on the dot. An hour and a half later, it would arrive in Medicine Hat.

Kate learned from her father that the fairgrounds were only a ten minute ride from the train station. She and Jimmy had decided to meet at the fairground stable at noon, in the stall her dad had reserved for Peppy, where she would change into Brian's clothes.

Kate was worried about one thing, though: Mr. Willis.

"Won't you get into trouble with your father?" she asked Jimmy.

"If your dad isn't angry, mine won't be, either," Jimmy said. "At least, not much."

"I don't think my dad will be," Kate said. "Oh, he might be upset with me at first. But Dad really wants a McGill cutting-horse at Medicine Hat. And now he'll have one!"

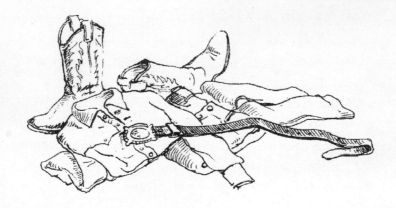

Journey to Medicine Hat

The day of the contest, Thursday, August 10th, dawned clear and cool. Kate and her mother and father ate breakfast by lamplight. Brian was still asleep.

Kate had time to run to the barn to give Chinook one last pat and to whisper "good luck!" in his ear.

Then she and her dad hurried to the car and bumped down the road to the cabin to pick up Mr. Willis.

The cabin was dark, too. But Mr. Willis and Jimmy were both standing on the front porch when the McGills arrived.

Mr. Willis climbed into the Model T, Jimmy raised

his hand to wave, and the two McGills and Joe Willis set off for Medicine Hat.

The yearly five-day fair was the most exciting thing that happened for miles around. The cutting-horse contest was only one of the contests there. There was bull-riding, bronco-riding, and calf-roping. There was also a livestock show, where ranchers could enter their best bulls and cows, and their pigs and chickens to be judged for prizes. There were contests for the tastiest pies, and the prettiest hooked rugs, and the biggest cabbages.

There was something for everyone in Medicine Hat. And it seemed as though practically everyone in southern Alberta was coming to see the show that day. In the town itself, Mr. McGill drove down a street hung with colorful banners that led to the fairgrounds. There, huge brown tents housed the exhibits and the livestock—Kate saw signs that read, "Cattle," "Sheep," and "Poultry." And finally she found the sign she was looking for: "Horse Stable." That's where she would be meeting Jimmy.

Beyond the tents lay the arena, a big, oval corral with high bleachers on both sides of it for the onlookers.

There were people everywhere, walking in and out of the tents, or grooming fat cattle under the trees, or adjusting the saddles on their horses.

"We'd better hurry," Mr. McGill said, pulling the Model T into an empty parking space. "The cutting is about to begin."

He and Kate and Joe Willis climbed into the bleachers in time to see the first grown-up ride into the arena to cut cattle. "This is Michael Dempsey," the rodeo announcer said over a loudspeaker. "He's come to us all the way from Calgary."

Mr. Dempsey was riding a red sorrel with a yellow mane and tail. The horse was bigger than Chinook, with longer legs and a longer head.

Kate had watched the cutting-horse contest in Medicine Hat many times before. But it was the first time she had studied it carefully, to figure out exactly how things worked.

The cattle herd was much larger than anything Chinook was used to. Kate counted twenty-five cows and big calves in the arena. And there were two riders to hold the herd. Once the cutter had chosen a calf and pushed it away from the herd, they held the remaining cattle behind him. Chinook had never seen herd holders. There were also two turnback men, to keep the calf from running away from the cutter, across the arena.

Then there was the crowd: people packed the

bleachers on either side of the arena. Chinook had never had anyone watching him, except Jimmy and the dogs, and now there would be hundreds.

Kate hoped her horse wouldn't be frightened by all of these differences. She began to wonder if maybe she hadn't bitten off more than she and Chinook could chew.

A whistle blew, and Michael Dempsey rode into the herd to choose a cow or calf to cut. He had just two-and-a-half minutes to show what his horse could do.

Kate listened to her father and Joe Willis talk about the cattle.

Mr. Willis said, "I think the spotted cow is blind in one eye. He ought to stay away from her. And that black calf looks wild."

Mr. McGill said, "That red calf is a good one. He's not too nervous, but he moves well—he would really let the cutter show off his horse."

But Mr. Dempsey chose a brown-and-white calf. He pushed it out of the herd, into the middle of the arena. The two herd holders kept the remaining cattle from moving up behind the horse. And the two turnback men saw to it that the calf didn't hightail it across the arena.

The cutting horse got down to business. And he

really did get down. The horse was so focused on the calf that he worked almost in a squat. The calf didn't make a move without the horse being right there with him, almost in his face.

"That sorrel horse is good!" said Mr. Willis.

Cutters lose points if they move their hands at all while the horse is working. Mr. Dempsey's left hand held the reins loosely. His right hand rested on the saddle horn.

After about a minute and a half, he raised the reins a bit to pull his horse away from the brown-and-white calf. Then he rode into the herd for a second time. Michael Dempsey had just started working a white cow when the whistle blew. His two-and-a-half minutes were up.

"Was it good for him to choose another cow to work?" Kate asked.

"I guess he felt that the first one was getting tired," said her father. Then he pointed at the two judges standing just outside the fence near the midpoint of the arena. "I wonder how they marked him," he said.

"I would have marked him high," said Mr. Willis.

"Is eighty points a perfect score?" Kate asked her dad.

"Eighty points for each judge," said Mr. McGill.

"With two judges, one hundred sixty points is perfect."

"But nobody is perfect," said Joe Willis. "High seventies is about as good as anyone gets."

Kate thought that some of the horses she saw in the grown-ups' cutting were pretty nearly perfect. The longer she watched, the more her stomach flip-flopped. Each horse seemed better than the last!

What if she had made a big mistake? What if she and Chinook froze in the arena? Or what if Kate fell off, like Brian? "I'll have gotten Jimmy—and myself—into a peck of trouble for nothing!" she thought.

"What time is it, Dad?" Kate asked.

Mr. McGill pulled out his pocket watch. "Almost twelve," he said.

Which meant that Jimmy and Chinook should be arriving at the horse barn—if everything went well! "I'm hungry," said Kate. "May I go to the sandwich tent?"

Her dad nodded. "Fine. But get back before one o'clock—that's when the cutting for first-timers' starts," he said.

"I'll see you then," said Kate. She added to herself, "Or at least *you'll* see *me*."

She climbed down from the bleachers. Once she had glanced over her shoulder to make sure her father wasn't watching her, Kate sprinted toward their car.

She grabbed Brian's gear out of the back. Then she raced to the horse barn as fast as she could.

The barn had two alleys running from one end to the other, with horse stalls on both sides of them. She hurried up the first alley, looking first one way and then the other—no Chinook, or Jimmy. She started searching down the second alley. She was beginning to wonder if they had made it at all. What if something had happened to them?!

Then Jimmy Willis stepped out of a stall into the alley and called, "Kate—finally! Where have you been?"

Chinook stuck his head over the stall door. When the horse saw Kate, he nickered. And he had never looked so good to her! Neither had Jimmy Willis, for that matter.

"I couldn't get away from my dad, and yours," Kate said to Jimmy, stroking Chinook's face. "Stand outside the door, so I can change into Brian's clothes."

Inside the stall, Kate kicked off her boots. As she pulled off her riding pants and pulled Brian's on, she asked Jimmy through the door, "Was the train ride okay? Did you have any trouble with Mr. Coulter, the engineer?" She didn't give him any time to answer before asking more questions: "How did Chinook act on the train? Was he scared? Stop it, Chinook," she added, giggling—the horse was nibbling at her hair.

Kate ran Brian's belt through the belt loops of the pants. She put her boots back on. Then she braided her hair into two quick, not-very-neat braids. She stuck the braids up under Brian's black hat.

Kate opened the stall door. "How do I look?" she asked worriedly.

Jimmy stared at her for a second or two. Then he said: "Brian McGill! I guess you made it, after all!"

"I couldn't have done it without you," Kate said.

CHAPTER THIRTEEN

And the Winner Is...

Kate didn't want to ride Chinook into the cutting arena cold. She and Jimmy led the horse over to an open field at the edge of the fairgrounds, where other riders were warming up their horses, too.

"Maybe this will keep us out of my dad's way," Kate said to Jimmy, glancing cautiously around for Mr. McGill's gray Stetson hat.

"And mine." said Jimmy.

At first, Chinook was a little hesitant. But once Kate climbed into the saddle and took hold of the reins, he settled down. For half an hour or so, they did circles and figure eights. "Taking the kinks out of Chinook," Jimmy called it.

Just as Kate was deciding that Chinook had had enough exercise, someone called to her: "Hey—Brian! Is that a new horse?"

Oh, no! It was Justin Robb!

"Hey!" was all Kate called back, hoping she sounded enough like Brian. She noticed that Justin wasn't riding Skyrocket—he was riding a new horse, too, a stocky brown horse. Now they seemed to be heading in her direction.

Kate quickly turned Chinook away. She trotted over to Jimmy, who was standing at the edge of the field.

"Who is that?" Jimmy asked, frowning past her.

"Justin Robb, one of our neighbors," Kate said hurriedly. "Let's get out of here!"

She slid off Chinook. Jimmy grabbed the reins. The three of them dodged into the milling crowd of fair-goers before Justin could reach them.

"Whew! That was close!" said Kate.

"Yeah, but it told us one thing," Jimmy said.

"What?" said Kate, still shaken.

"You look enough like Brian today to get away with this!" said Jimmy.

Then they overheard a man saying, "It's almost one o'clock."

"It's almost time for Chinook and me!" Kate said,

taking a deep breath.

She and Jimmy led Chinook to the back of the arena, and stayed well out of sight behind a loading chute. Over the loudspeaker, the announcer said, "Good afternoon, ladies and gentlemen. The boys' cutting contest is about to begin. We're starting out with the first-timers' class—it's the first time out for either the horses, or the boys, or both. And our first contestant is Harlan Forbes, on a nice-looking paint horse."

For Kate, the two-and-a-half minutes that Harlan Forbes rode seemed like two-and-a-half seconds, two-and-a-half seconds until she might be riding herself. After the final whistle, she stopped breathing altogether, waiting to hear if Brian's name would be called out.

One boy rode, two boys, three, six . . .

When the sixth boy left the arena, the announcer said, "Next we'll be watching Brian McGill, from the McGill ranch—he'll be riding Peppy."

"Come on, Kate," Jimmy said to her. "That's you."

Kate was frozen on her horse. She couldn't move. Not even her mind was working.

But Jimmy grabbed the reins and ran with Chinook to the gate into the arena.

"You'll be fine," he told Kate. "Just let Chinook get

his work done. Good luck!"

A man pushed the gate open so that Kate and Chinook could walk through it. Jimmy gave the horse a pat on the rump . . . and then they were inside the arena. The man closed the gate behind them.

The arena looked huge. Thousands of eyes were focused on Kate and her horse. And one pair of those eyes belonged to her father. Kate wondered what he was thinking right about now . . .

"Make him proud!" Kate said to herself. "This is what you wanted, remember?"

She glanced down at Chinook's little ears—they were already pointed straight at the herd of cattle bunched together at the far end of the pen. Chinook's mind was on his business. She had better get hers on it, too!

Kate nudged Chinook with her legs. They walked past the two turnback men, toward the herd. About twenty feet away from the cattle, Kate stopped her horse for a second to study them. The red calf that her father had talked about was standing behind a cow on the left side of the herd . . .

The whistle blew.

Barely squeezing Chinook with her legs, Kate nudged him forward to push the red calf farther to the left. A few steps more, and the calf was separated from the rest of the herd.

There were plenty of things for Kate to remember: To hold the reins loosely with her left hand. To rest her right hand on the saddle horn. To sit straight in the saddle.

Her legs hung straight down from her hips, with a little bend in the knees. And Kate tried to stay as relaxed as she could. If her muscles tensed up, Chinook would feel it, and he would tighten up, too.

Kate had to leave the cutting to Chinook. She couldn't direct him in any way without losing points. Chinook didn't let her down—he worked with all his heart.

With the two turnback riders, Chinook could stay tighter on the calf than he ever had in practice. The red calf couldn't take a step to the right or the left without Chinook doing the same.

In a way, it was the longest two-and-a-half minutes of Kate's life.

In another way, it was the shortest. When the final whistle blew, and Kate pulled her horse away from the calf, she wished she could have shown Chinook off for the rest of the afternoon!

The crowd seemed to want that, too. Their applause was like thunder!

"A mighty good horse, and a mighty good ride

from a young fellow named Brian McGill!" boomed the announcer.

People were still clapping when Kate and Chinook rode through the gate. Kate began to look around for Jimmy . . . and spotted him sandwiched between two men: Mr. Willis and her father!

She trotted Chinook straight over to them. Before either one could say anything, Kate blurted out, "Please don't be mad at Jimmy. This was all my idea! Chinook is so good at cutting, it just wasn't fair that he couldn't be in the contest. After Brian got hurt, I convinced Jimmy to bring Chinook on the train, and I borrowed some of Brian's clothes, and . . ."

"Slow down, slow down, Katie," Mr. McGill said, starting to laugh. "I'm not mad at Jimmy. As I told Joe, I was sure this whole thing was your idea. And I'm not mad at you, either. In fact, I'm proud enough to burst about the job you've done training Chinook!"

Kate was so pleased that all she could say was, "You are?"

"I am," said Mr. McGill. "But let's watch the rest of the contest. Justin Robb is about to ride."

As the McGills and the Willises looked on from outside the arena, Justin Robb and the brown horse moved into the herd. But Justin made a big mistake. He chose the spotted cow with a blind eye.

If her blind side was toward the brown horse, the cow couldn't see which way the horse was moving. And she wasn't afraid of what she couldn't see. So she didn't stop or turn away, not even when the horse was right on top of her.

Before a minute was up, Justin had lost her. And losing his cow lost Justin a lot of points.

He chose another cow. But he couldn't work it long enough to make up for the points he had lost. The whistle blew all too soon.

Five more boys rode, and then it was over. The two judges met in the arena to compare notes and add up their scores. Then they walked to the announcer's booth to give the results.

"We've got the names of the winners here, folks," the rodeo announcer said over the loudspeaker. "Third place goes to Harlan Forbes from Red Deer Ranch. Harlan, come out here and get your prize."

The crowd clapped as the boy rode his paint horse into the arena to pick up his trophy from the judges.

"Second place was taken by Chester Martin from over near Purple Springs! Chester, congratulations!" said the announcer.

Chester Martin was riding a pretty bay horse with black stockings. The teenager waved his trophy in the air.

Kate was getting more and more nervous. She had thought she and Chinook might win third place. Or maybe second, if they were really lucky. But first place, first time out for both of them? She didn't think so.

"Sorry, Chinook," she murmured to her horse. "Anyway, we gave it our best."

Suddenly the announcer boomed: "And first place for the first-timers' class for boys eighteen and under goes to . . . BRIAN MCGILL! Ride in here, Brian, so we can get a look at you, and at that talented horse of yours—his name is Peppy, isn't it?"

"No!" Jimmy Willis yelled as loud as he could from the gate. "It's Chinook!"

"CHINOOK!" Mr. McGill and Mr. Willis both shouted.

"Chinook!" said the announcer. "That's a fine Canadian name."

Kate and Chinook had won first place? Kate was frozen again! But her dad pulled the gate open for her, and joked, "Get in there, before they change their minds!"

As Kate and Chinook trotted across the arena, the applause thundered around them. One of the judges held up a big silver trophy and said to Kate, "You and your horse did a great job out there, son." He handed the trophy to her.

Kate thought for a second. Then she pulled off Brian's hat and let her braids hang down for everybody to see.

"I'm a girl," she said to the judges. "Kate McGill."

At the same time, the announcer shouted: "She's a girl!"

"This contest is . . . is for boys!" the other judge said, sounding flustered. And he reached out to take the trophy back.

But by then Mr. McGill was standing beside Kate and Chinook. "Kate and her horse won the contest, fair and square!" Mr. McGill boomed.

The crowd must have agreed with him, because people started calling out, "Good for you!" and "She's the winner!" and "She deserves that trophy—she made the best ride!"

The announcer said, "For the first time, a girl has ridden in the Medicine Hat cutting-horse contest! Not only ridden in it, but she has won *first place*! I have a feeling that it's not the last time we'll be seeing . . . what's your name again, young lady?"

Kate called out loud and clear: "Kate—Kate McGill! And this is Chinook!"

"Kate and Chinook!" boomed the announcer. "I'm sure we'll see you next year!"

"You bet you will!" said Kate, patting Chinook's neck.

Chinook bobbed his head and nickered softly in agreement.

FACTS
ABOUT THE BREED

You probably know a lot about Quarter Horses from reading this book. Here are some more interesting facts about this popular breed.

∩ Quarter Horses generally stand between 15 and 16 hands high. Instead of using feet and inches, all horses are measured in hands. A hand is equal to four inches.

∩ Quarter Horses are usually chestnut (reddish brown all over) or bay (brown with a black mane, tail, and lower leg). A registered Quarter Horse can be of any color.

∩ A horse cannot be registered with the American Quarter Horse Association if it has any white on its legs or body above the knees. White on the face is acceptable, but the whole face must not be white.

∩ Quarter Horses are famous for their heavily muscled hind quarters. These muscles allow the Quarter Horse to take off at a gallop from a standing start. Quarter Horses are often photographed from behind to show off these strong muscles.

∩ Quarter Horses were developed from horses imported from England to Virginia and North and South Carolina in the early 1600s. Those horses, who were probably of Arabian, English, and Barb ancestry, were crossed with the Spanish horses that were already in America.

∩ Although the Quarter Horse was developed early in American history, the American Quarter Horse Association was not founded until 1940.

∩ In the late 1700s, Quarter Horses were called "Celebrated American Quarter-mile Running Horses" or "C.A.Q.R.H." They got this name because they are unbeatable at distances of a quarter mile or less.

∩ Before the foundation of the American Quarter Horse Association, Quarter Horses were know by several different names, including "Steeldusts" and "Billys."

∩ Some Quarter Horse fans believe that the Quarter Horse is the most popular horse in the world. In fact, the American Quarter Horse Association is the largest horse registry in the world with over three million entries.

∩ The Quarter Horse's powerful hind quarters also make it a great cutting horse. While cutting, or separating a cow from the herd, a horse needs not only to stop and start quickly, but also to turn on a dime. The Quarter Horse can do that, and at high speed, thanks to its strongly muscled rump and thighs.

∩ Quarter Horses are favorites among cowboys because of their "cow sense" and cutting abilities. They also excel at roping, another important cattle ranch skill, and barrel racing, a popular Western sport.

∩ Although Thoroughbred racing has stolen some of the limelight from the Quarter Horse, Quarter Horse racing is still popular. The All-American Futurity, held every year at Ruidoso Downs, New Mexico, is one of the world's richest horse races. A winner at this race can take home as much as one million dollars.

∩ A good Quarter Horse can run the quarter mile (440 yards) in 21 seconds or less.

∩ A Quarter Horse was the star of the 1994 film *Black Beauty*. Docs Keepin Time, a registered American Quarter Horse, won a Silver Spurs Award for outstanding achievement in entertainment for his performance in the film.

∩ Quarter Horses are also used for general pleasure riding, trail riding, hunting, and jumping. They even perform in the dressage ring. Their athletic ability, coupled with their calm disposition make the Quarter Horse an excellent all-round horse. No wonder they are among the most popular horses in the world!